So Say The Little Monkeys

by **Nancy Van Laan**   pictures by **Yumi Heo**

Harcourt

Orlando   Boston   Dallas   Chicago   San Diego

Visit *The Learning Site!*
www.harcourtschool.com

For my sister, Julie, and her menagerie
—N. V. L.

For my son, Auden
—Y. H.

This edition is published by special arrangement with Atheneum Books for Young Readers, Simon & Schuster Children's Publishing Division.

Grateful acknowledgment is made to Atheneum Books for Young Readers, Simon &Schuster Children's Publishing Division for permission to reprint *So Say the Little Monkeys* by Nancy Van Laan, illustrated by Yumi Heo. Text copyright © 1998 by Nancy Van Laan; illustrations copyright © 1998 by Yumi Heo.

Printed in the United States of America

ISBN 0-15-313405-4

13 14 15 179 06 05 04

A NOTE ABOUT THE STORY

In Brazil, a huge country in South America, there are many rivers. Second in size to the Amazon is the Rio Negro, the Black River, which got its name from its dark waters, black as coal.

In the trees along its banks live tiny monkeys, which the Indians call "blackmouths." Their mouths are as dark as the waters of the river. These monkeys live in the tall palms which are full of sharp thorns. Unlike the birds, the monkeys do not make any type of permanent home. Even though the thorns must be very uncomfortable, they sleep on top of them each night. The Indians who live there created an amusing tale to explain why this is so.

Near the deep black waters
of a dark, cool river,
tiny, tiny monkeys
jabber in the sun.

They swing, WHEEEE, over here.

They swing, WHEEEE, over there.

They sing, "Jibba jibba jabba,"

as they jump and run.

JUMP, JABBA JABBA,

RUN, JABBA JABBA,

Tiny, tiny monkeys having fun!

As they climb tall trees
full of sharp, sharp thorns,
their tiny black mouths
shriek, "OW OW OW!"

Still they climb, UP-UP!
And they slide, DOWN-DOWN!
They sing, "Jibba jibba jabba,"
swinging round and round.

JUMP, JABBA JABBA,
RUN, JABBA JABBA,
SLIDE, JABBA JABBA,
Tiny, tiny monkeys having fun!

At the end of the day,
when it's time to rest,
most others go to
their warm, cozy nests.

Toucan snuggles deep
in a dry tree hole.
Armadillo burrows
underground like a mole.

But the tiny, tiny monkeys
creep, creep, creep,
up thorny, thorny trees
where they try to sleep.

There's an OUCH over there.
There's an OUCH over here.
They cry, "Jabba jabba,"
as the rain draws near.

Comes the rain, PLINKA PLINKA.
Comes the wind, WOOYA WOOYA.
"EEEYI!" cry the monkeys.
"It's c-cold out here!"

Tiny, tiny monkeys,
soaked to the bone,
chatter to each other,
"L-let's b-build us a home!"

But when the next day dawns,
and the sun comes out,
Tiny, tiny monkeys
screech and shout.

They swing, WHEEEE, over here.
They swing, WHEEEE, over there.
They sing, "Jibba jibba jabba,"
as they jump and run.

JUMP, JABBA JABBA,
RUN, JABBA JABBA,
SLIDE, JABBA JABBA,
SCREECH, JABBA JABBA,
SHOUT, JABBA JABBA,
Tiny, tiny monkeys having fun!

Then one monkey says,
"Let's gather wood!"
"Yes! Yes!" howl the others.
"We really should."

With a leap and a shriek,
they pick, pick, pick,
a leaf or a twig
or a fat, fat stick.

But when two monkeys find
ripe bananas in a bunch,
all the tiny monkeys
stop and MUNCH MUNCH MUNCH.

They swing, WHEEEE, over here.
They swing, WHEEEE, over there.
They sing, "Jibba jibba jabba,"
as they jump and run.

JUMP, JABBA JABBA,
RUN, JABBA JABBA,
SLIDE, JABBA JABBA,
SCREECH, JABBA JABBA,
SHOUT, JABBA JABBA,
MUNCH, JABBA JABBA,
Tiny, tiny monkeys having fun!

Night falls again
as the sun goes down,
and they huddle all together
when the rain starts to pound.

Comes the rain, PLINKA PLINKA.
Comes the wind, WOOYA WOOYA.
Comes the jaguar, GURR-YUH GURR-YUH.
Monkeys run, run, run!

Now each tired monkey
is wishing for a bed—
"We should have built a house,
just like we said!"

But what do you think
they *do* the next day?
Do they build a warm nest?
Or do they eat and play?

They swing, WHEEEE, over here.
They swing, WHEEEE, over there.
They sing, "Amanha—tomorrow!"
as they jump and run.
JUMP, JABBA JABBA,
RUN, JABBA JABBA,
SLIDE, JABBA JABBA,
SCREECH, JABBA JABBA,
SHOUT, JABBA JABBA,
MUNCH, JABBA JABBA,
SWING, JABBA JABBA,
SING, JABBA JABBA.

Amanha—tomorrow, will it *ever* come?